Farm
Alphabet Book

Farm
Alphabet Book

Jane Miller

SCHOLASTIC BOOK SERVICES
New York Toronto London Auckland Sydney Tokyo

ISBN: 0-590-31991-4

12 11 10 9 8 7 6 5 4 3 2 1   9   1 2 3 4 5 6/8
Printed in the U.S.A.   09

To Jean Brooker who started the whole idea.

A
a

apple

Apples are picked in the late summer and autumn, when they are ripe.

Bb

bull

A bull is a calf's father.
It is a large, strong animal.

Cc

calf

A calf is a young cow or young bull.

D d

donkey

Donkeys
graze in
the fields
when they
are not
pulling carts.

E e

egg

Birds lay
eggs.
These eggs
were laid
by a hen.

Ff

foal

A foal is a young horse.
Its mother is a mare.
Its father is a stallion.

G g

goat

A young goat
is a kid.
Its mother is
a nanny goat.
Its father is
a billy goat.

H
h

hen

A hen is the
mother of
a chick.
The chick's
father is
a rooster.

I i

incubator

An incubator
keeps eggs
warm.
After 21 days
chicks
hatch out
of the eggs.

Jj

jam

Jam is made from fruit
boiled with sugar and water.

K
k

kitten

A kitten is
a young cat.

Ll

lamb

A lamb is a young sheep.
Its mother is a ewe.
Its father is a ram.

Mm

mouse

A mouse sleeps during the day and finds its food at night.

N
n

nest

Nests are
built by birds.
Birds lay their
eggs in nests.
This is a
coot's nest.

O o

orchard

Fruit trees
grow in
orchards.

P p

pig

This mother pig
is called a sow.
A father pig is a boar.
A young pig is a piglet.

Q
q

quill

A quill is a
large feather.
It grows in
a bird's wing
or tail.
A quill can be
used as a pen.

R r

rabbit

Tame rabbits are kept as pets. Wild rabbits live in burrows under the ground.

S s

swan

A mother
swan teaches
her cygnets
to swim
as soon
as they are
hatched.

Tt

tractor

Tractors pull machines
on the farm.

Uu

umbrella

Umbrellas keep people dry when it rains.

V v

vegetable

Vegetables
are grown
on farms and
in gardens.

W
W

web

Webs are
spun by
spiders.
The webs catch
insects for
the spiders
to eat.

X x

x

X shows that this
sheep and lamb
belong to the farmer.

Yy

yolk

A yolk is the yellow part of an egg.

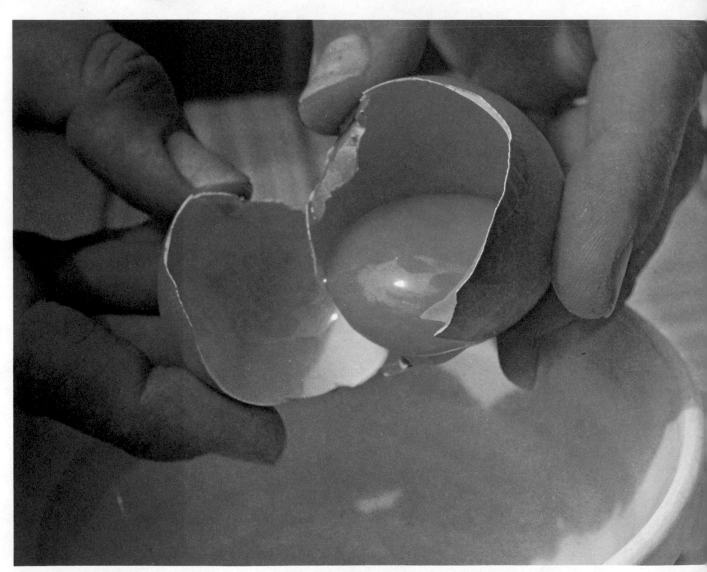

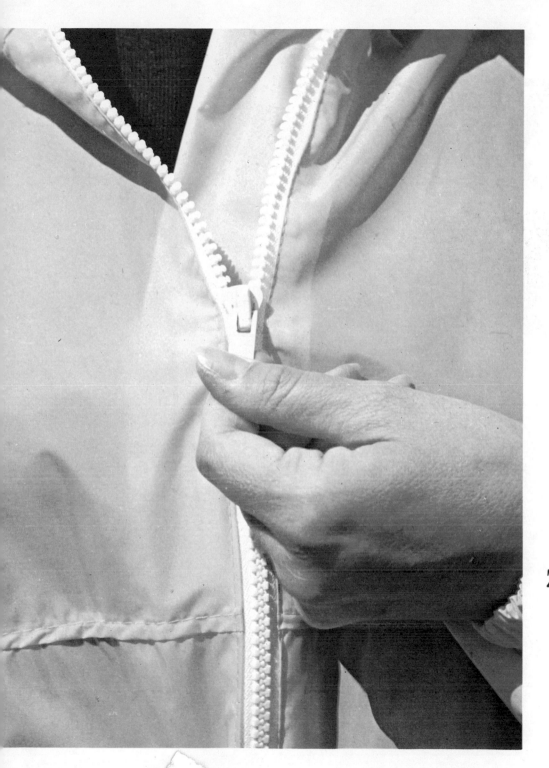

Z z

zipper

Zippers open
and close
all kinds
of clothes
worn on
the farm.